THE LIBRARY OF UNREQUITED LOVE

"Funny, sad and agreeably discursive . . . A very accomplished and delightful debut, a book which makes one look forward to what Divry will write next, and which even invites one to engage in that rash practice – prophesying a brilliant future for the author"

ALLAN MASSIE, *Scotsman*

"Sophie Divry brilliantly captures the voice of a frustrated lady librarian past her prime, trapped in her bookworm world . . . We're in Anita Brookner territory here . . . Next time you go to the library, you might find yourself looking at that mousy librarian twice"

KATIE LAW, *Evening Standard*

"A sharply clever stream of conciousness diatribe, a sad and funny potrait of a women, and a hymn of praise to books and libraries"

Good Book Guide

"Short but sweet; an interesting monologue from an engaging character with lots to say" *We Love this Book*

"A wonderful novella filled with remarkable, striking observations about books, libraries, love and life . . . A lovely little book that will resonate with keen readers" *The Little Reader Library*

"I smiled, I laughed, I shook my head with irritation, I nodded vigorously in agreement, and I had a thoroughly stimulating two hours in the Library of Unrequited Love" *Vulpes Libris*

"I would definitely recommend every book-lover give *The Library of Unrequited Love* a whirl . . . With a short, quirky debut like this I am very much looking forward to seeing what Sophie Divry comes up with next" *Savidge Reads*

SOPHIE DIVRY lives in Lyon. She likes aubergines, olive oil and her mother's homemade jam. She hates cars, is a feminist and has a phobia about open doors. She likes swimming in the sea, lakes or rivers, but does not like buying a book without knowing what's inside it. *The Library of Unrequited Love* is her first novel.

SIÂN REYNOLDS is a past winner of the Scott Moncrieff Translation prize, and has translated many French writers, from Fernand Braudel to Fred Vargas. She lives in Edinburgh.

SOPHIE DIVRY

THE LIBRARY OF
UNREQUITED LOVE

Translated from the French by
Siân Reynolds

MACLEHOSE PRESS
QUERCUS · LONDON

First published in the French language as *La Cote 400*
by Les Éditions Les Allusifs, Montréal, 2010
First published in English in 2013 by MacLehose Press
This paperback edition published in 2014 by

MacLehose Press
an imprint of Quercus
55 Baker Street
7th Floor, South Block
London W1U 8EW

A CIP catalogue record for this book is available
from the British Library.

ISBN (MMP) 978 1 78087 051 9
ISBN (Ebook) 978 1 78087 052 6

10 9 8 7 6 5 4 3 2 1

Designed and typeset in Albertina by Libanus Press, Marlborough
Printed and bound in Great Britain by Clays Ltd, St Ives plc

To all those men and women who will always find a place
for themselves in a library more easily than in society,
I dedicate this entertainment

Reading is, with friendship, one of the surest contributions
to the work of grieving. It helps us, more generally, to grieve
for the limitations of our life, the limitations
of the human condition

DIDIER ANZIEU, *Le Corps de l'Oeuvre*

Nobody sees me, that's my problem. Even in the street, people bump into me and say, "Oh, sorry, didn't see you." The invisible woman, that's who I am, the invisible woman, the one in charge of the Geography section. Ah, yes, now you've remembered who I am, of course. Oh there it is, thanks very much, that was quick of you. *Existentialism Is a Humanism* has no business down here in my basement, we don't have philosophy on this level. It suits the eggheads on the ground floor. I'll give it back to them, they'll be pleased, they've been looking for it for ages up there. See, you really are a big help. Anyway, I'm not allowed to open the doors for you, it would mean calling the security people, it's too dangerous. Yes, it is, it's dangerous, because it would be unprecedented, first time ever. And in a library, one should never draw attention to oneself. If you attract attention, you'll disturb people. You can just stay here with me while I get my reading room ready. I've more books to shelve. And since you're so efficient, can you take out of the History section all the geography books that readers have shoved in there? Go on, don't complain: sorting, rearranging, sleep well, at least, down here? No? You were scared? Oh, but it's very quiet. I like the peace and quiet, I find it reassuring. But that's how I am, I need precision and routine. I could never work in a railway station: too much going on and the very idea that a train was going to be late would give me a panic attack. Anyway, I never take the train nowadays, I'm too old for that. I don't drive either, it's too dangerous and I hate car parks, I like old-fashioned beauty. Just the very idea of getting on the slip road to a motorway gives me palpitations. Don't stay standing up like that, I'll get you a coffee. I always bring a Thermos of coffee when I come in early. Drink up, it'll make you feel better. Believe me. Now just sit down there and don't bother me again, or I'll get stressed. Even in small-town libraries like this, people make terrible mistakes in their shelving. It drives me up the wall, it's a sign of how pathetic they are. Not only do they shut absent-minded readers into my basement at night, but they shelve the books all wrong as well. Because, theoretically, whether you're in Paris, Marseille, Cahors, Mazamet or Dompierre-sur-Besbre, you ought to be able to find the same book in the same place. See, take a classic work of sociology, Émile Durkheim's *The Division of Labour in Society*. Well, there it is, shelfmark 301. Next to *Suicide*. That's another great classic by Durkheim: *Suicide*. Same author, same shelfmark: 301 DUR. Works every time. Can't go wrong. The man who invented this system, his name was Melvil Dewey. He's our founding father, for all us librarians. Just a little guy from a poor family somewhere in America, and he was only twenty-one when he thought up the most famous classification system in the world. Dewey is the Mendeleev of librarians. Not the Periodic Table of Elements, but the classification of areas of culture. His stroke of genius was to divide up the areas of knowledge under ten broad headings he called "classes": 000 for general works, 100 for philosophy, 200 for religions. 300 for social sciences, 400 for languages, 500 for mathematics, 600 for technology, 700 for fine art, 800 for literature, 900 for history and geography – and everything else they couldn't classify ends up here in the basement too. Yes, sorry, my coffee is always too strong, that way I don't get obsessed at any rate. I'm sure he was one of those people who can't get to sleep unless their slippers are neatly lined up at the foot of the bed and the kitchen sink has been completely scoured. I understand him, I'm the same myself. This was someone who devoted his entire life to libraries, his existence revolved around books, that was it. Since he was American, and you know how practical they are, Dewey set up a cabinet-making firm to manufacture library furniture, the *Library Bureau Company*, pardon my English pronunciation. The company still exists today. Oh, that's so American. It sells really good quality furniture. They have a few pieces in Paris, at the library at Beaubourg, the Pompidou Centre. This library can't afford them, of course, our furniture is shoddy stuff. I've told the Head Librarian, and indeed the Mayor, that cheap bookcases aren't good enough, but what can I say, they couldn't care less. Anyway, I don't count for anything. No-one listens to me. I'm totally invisible. In fact, if I hadn't deliberately made a noise just now when I arrived, you'd still be fast asleep, you wouldn't have been disturbed. I'm sorry to have interrupted that. But what really gets me, a huge mistake, is moving Languages from 400 to 800. What have they put there instead? Nothing. So shelfmark 400 is now unoccupied, it's just empty. You agree with me, don't you, it's ridiculous. It makes my head spin, having a vacant shelfmark. What's going to be put there? What domain of culture and human knowledge that we haven't properly valued is going to take it over in the future? I prefer not to think about this unoccupied shelfmark, it frightens me. Like swimming far out to sea. I've only done that once, in the days when I was still taking holidays. More than fifteen years ago. Nowadays I don't go on holiday, not even weekends, I can't stand leisure. There's no space for leisure in life. You're either going up or down, end of story. And at a certain point in your life, you have to decide what you want to do with your time. Well, as I was saying, I was younger then. I'd been dragged onto a boat, I was taken sailing, and suddenly they were all in wetsuits and over the side. I jumped in too, because I didn't want to be the only one left on deck. But I wasn't happy, we were out of sight of the coast. And suddenly, thinking how deep it was under my feet, I had a panic attack. Brr, I nearly drowned, it still makes me shiver. Ghastly things, holidays! Give me some of that coffee, that'll make me feel better. The idea of leaving an empty shelfmark is so abysmally stupid. It really upsets me. They should never have laid a finger on the Dewey System. Because now, instead of calling it the Dewey Decimal Classification, they call it "the universal classification". That gets people going, I can tell you. Some of my colleagues spend their lives working out tiny nuances in the shelfmarks, classifying, numbering, declassifying, de-numbering. And all for the sake of order, hierarchy, tidiness. Oh, don't think I'm complaining. I like my job. Well, O.K., I confess, when I began studying, I didn't mean to become a librarian. I wanted to be a secondary school teacher, but I failed the teaching diploma. So now here I am, an assembly line worker, shelving books, issuing them, beep-beep. I'm nobody, nothing at all. But no, no, I'm not complaining. At least I don't have to shout all day at a lot of out-of-control schoolchildren. I have a quiet life. I work here Tuesday to Saturday, ten till five, think of those of us who have to work down here. Architects never think of anything, in my opinion anyway. I know quite a bit about architects, because I see them regularly poking about in this section. I never offer to help them, no, never. The first architect, or student of architecture, who comes along, with his silly glasses and portfolio, pays the price for the rest of them. They won't get any advice, not a smile, *niet, nada*. I believe in collective punishment. It's only fair. Whoever designed this stuffy basement condemned me, arbitrarily and definitively, to live in a dungeon, so I persecute them all in return. I get my revenge when I make them go up and down to different floors a few times before finding the right book, or when I annoy them with my trolley while they're trying to concentrate on their work, or when I keep trying to open one of their badly designed windows, or turn the air conditioning on or off. I harass them, yes, that's right. Don't look at me with those big eyes, I know when to stop. Nobody notices my little game. And anyway, you can't trust the readers an inch. I don't mean you personally, I'm speaking in general:

here to study. I watch him. That's all, it doesn't go any further. He's very intelligent. He's doing some serious research. I only have a first degree. Anyway. I was thinking (you have plenty of time to think in this job) and I told myself that I could never fall for someone who was less well educated than me. The men who carry the books from the stacks for us, for instance, they can still make the odd remark to me, well in fact they don't do that so much now, but even when they did, just little remarks or winks, I tell you, I hardly bothered looking at them. Not intellectual enough. To appeal to me, a man can be shorter than me or taller, richer or poorer, older or younger, nothing's an obstacle, I'm open-minded, you see. But he has to be more intelligent. And he has to be clean-shaven, no stubble, I hate scruffy people. My young researcher is very well turned out. His name's Martin. The first time I saw him, I'd just got off the bus at my usual stop, avenue Salengro, and I was walking along the pavement towards the new entrance to the library, opposite the little shopping centre. At first, I didn't pay any attention, it was just someone walking ahead of me,

Yes, that was a good point, I admit. I hadn't seen his face yet, but I was already imagining that he had a high forehead, dreamy eyes and a determined mouth. When we reached the market place, he didn't turn off to the shopping centre: no, he kept on going towards the library, like me. Then I realized it was the back of his neck that had captivated me, right from the start. Because is there anything more fascinating about a person than a beautiful neck seen from behind? The back of the neck is a promise, summing up the whole person through their most intimate feature. Yes, intimate. It's the part of your body you can never see yourself. A few inches of neck, with a trace of down, exposed to the sky, the back of the head, the last goodbye, the far side of the mind? Well, the back of Martin's neck is all of that. His square shoulders are a perfect setting for the upward sweep of his head, his curly hair caresses those few inches of skin, as if to soften his apparent solidity: a gentle and promising balance, so one already senses the strength of the body and the intelligence of the soul. How I admired him that day. Then, of course, I got to see his face. It's a marvellous

I don't dare invite him. I'm afraid I never will have the courage either. I don't want to disturb him in his work. And anyway, he doesn't come all that often, about once a week perhaps. The rest of the time, he must be at the University Library. Well, naturally, a local council library isn't a cultural El Dorado. Mind you, we've done well to get this far: more than two hundred thousand books available to borrow, it might never have happened. To get a public library in a little provincial town like this took centuries. And his nibs the Mayor isn't over-fond of us either. We never see him here, in fact, or anyone from his family. So apart from people like you, who are capable of falling asleep in a reading room, who comes here? Not that many people. They're so ungrateful. When you think of all the trouble it took to reach this point. Because if you care to look more closely into the history of libraries, who could have collected all these books so methodically? Not country bumpkins like you, let me tell you. You don't work on a farm, do you? Sorry, thought you did. But anyway, I don't need to see your tax return to see that unlike those kings and monks and nobles, people with power, in short, you wouldn't have been able to collect thousands of books. Take Cardinal Mazarin for instance, seventeenth century: he had forty thousand books in his personal library in Paris. Nice little collection. And one day, he decided to open it to the public. That was pretty good going, for a cardinal. Still, we shouldn't be fooled: what mattered most to him was the prestige it brought him. The building got to be called "the Mazarine". He was as proud as punch, our cardinal. Well, after all, books are like carriages, the whole point is to show off. True culture for rich people doesn't come till later, it creeps up on them, and it's not well regarded. In his case, it took the shape of an admirable man called Gabriel Naudé. A talented little commoner, who started off wanting to be a doctor, but he fell in love with the cardinal's books, so he became his head librarian. When the weather was overcast, you couldn't see a thing inside the poky Mazarine, it was worse than here. But they had an excuse, it was early days. Impressive early days. Gabriel Naudé there and then defined a dozen categories: theology, philosophy, history and so on, and shelfmark, the librarian can have really interesting conversations with the readers. In 1989, the Bicentennial, these books were flying off the shelves. They're lucky, the people in charge of History. Because if you're working in Geography you can wait for ever for a reader to ask you to suggest a book for holiday reading ... "Peasant revolts in the Poitiers region in the reign of Louis XV". Not easy to start a conversation about that. In any case, French history before the Revolution – I might have read about a hundred books on it, but I can't get my head round it. Well, is there anyone who can? Really? Charlemagne a bit, Joan of Arc perhaps, but honestly before the Revolution, nobody actually cares about it. It all seems a very long time ago, all that old stuff. Go on, admit it, I won't blame you. And yet the people who lived in the *ancien régime*, they weren't stupid at all, they respected books, especially after the Renaissance, with the invention of printing, not to mention the reformation and all those monomaniacs with their translations of the Bible, but it was all very elitist. The peasants, the poor, the Third Estate, the public, nobody bothered about them. That's why people like me, from humble backgrounds, we don't feel concerned about anything much before the Revolution. That's how it was. And it could have stayed that way. No movement. Apart from, excuse me while I have a little laugh, a few peasant revolts in the Poitiers region. And then wham! The Revolution. What I admire about our revolutionaries is their capacity for organization. Robespierre was the least head-in-the-air person in history. Him and his colleagues, they were quite right to issue all those thousands of laws and decrees and orders. Because it really needed a good clean-out. Before that it was all privileges, tithes, salt tax, plumed hats. With their holy days for Saint Eustace and Saint Eulalia, different weights and measures in every parish in France, people speaking dialects nobody could understand ten miles away, it was total chaos. And if you were faced with that anarchy, you needed some beautiful, clear and popular rationality. So they went right at it, no shilly-shallying. My greatest regret is that they gave up on the republican calendar when it was perfectly rational: instead of our fifty-two weeks that never work out the same from year to the whole of Europe. That's another reason I don't go travelling. Napoleon's always been there first. I can't stand it. And when I say total mayhem, I'm being polite. In fact, he destroyed everything: looted, burned, pillaged. Who was the real gravedigger of the Revolution? Napoleon. A barbarian and a tyrant. Encouraging the people to read wasn't what he was about, he preferred to get a whole generation of young men massacred marching through the snow. Did you know that the Napoleonic wars killed more Frenchmen than the First World War? No, of course not. You don't learn stuff like that on T.V., you learn it here, by reading the history periodicals we subscribe to. A barbarian, that's what he was, a dictator. When I see the number of books that come out every year about that uncivilized little runt, I can't understand the fascination with Napoleon, it's appalling, I just don't get it. And we have this nice periodicals room, very comfortable. But I'm probably talking too much. I wouldn't dare go on like this to Martin. That's where I'm contradictory: I like men who are more intelligent than me, but the idea that they might think me stupid paralyses me. And I might have read a hundred or more books on the Revolution, I still don't know everything about it either. So where was I? Oh yes, after that, came Louis-Philippe, who was a lot more democratic than he gets credit for, and he would have liked every region to have a library. But it didn't happen. That's no reason to be unfair about Louis-Philippe, he wasn't that bad. And I like a man with sideburns. I think Martin would be even better-looking if he had sideburns. Although it was his intelligence that first attracted me, I still allow myself to imagine: ah, Martin with sideburns. Well. Anyway. Now the Third Republic *did* try to make books available to everyone, but the First World War didn't help. It was total chaos. The filth, the trenches, the mud, the blood, the barbed wire. What a nightmare, you have to say. The guillotine was much more civilized. A heart-breaker, the Great War, what a step backwards for humanity, shelfmark 944.855. Durkheim lost his son to it and his young disciples, a terrible disaster for science. That's the way it is: wars always kill the sons, never the fathers who took the decisions. And once we got ourselves out of brilliant, that's my boy, Eugène. But it wasn't until after the Liberation in '44 that things really changed. From then on, they started to take some notice of the people. The Americans, who looked down on us while they were showering us with money, wanted to tell us all about public libraries. But at that point we said: "Stop! We've read Eugène Morel, we know exactly what to do, thanks." You'll have to forgive me. I come from a very ordinary background, so I know exactly what I owe and who I owe it to, I was the first person in my family to get as far as the *baccalauréat*. So you can't fool me. In the 1970s, when I started work, it was all still going full blast. People had the ideal of public service in those days. Not like now, with the youth who go straight to the comic book shelves, they don't see me, they don't even bother to reply when I say good morning. Then we had the social-ists in power in 1981, and all that. But, excuse me, we didn't have to wait for them to roll up either, before getting the library at Beaubourg, the Pompidou Centre. Open every night till 10.00 p.m. So people *could* have read books. If they could be bothered. Because, if I'm yes, I do suffer. The worst thing is getting these compulsive obsessions. They're always at me. I just have to see a book shoved in the wrong way on a shelf, sticking out, or drawing attention to itself, a bit too attractive perhaps, like that one over there, for me to . . . I'm afraid it's going to fall out, I'm afraid it's too noticeable, I can't concentrate now . . . or speak . . . until . . . Excuse me. I must just put it back in the right place. There. It doesn't stand out now. It *was* going to fall, wasn't it? Well, maybe I'm exaggerating. I get a bit stressed out with all these books to keep in order, and at the same time it calms me down being here. I'll tell you, I'm not ashamed, the library works like an anaesthetic for my hang-ups. Because when I first arrived in his town, I was in a terrible state. I'd just left Paris. I get here, in the depths of the provinces, I settle in. Or rather *we* settle in. Because I didn't come alone, you see. I wouldn't have dreamed of coming on my own to a town like this. I agreed to the move, because I made the mistake of falling in love. Big mistake. I can't understand the perennial fascination people nowadays have with love. It's a waste of time, it's a childish, tiring, that I was interested in it. I just got, pardon my language, the shitty job nobody else wanted. A very downmarket section, if you like. I stayed there three years. Then they moved me to Geography. And ever since, I've been hoping to get to my favourite section, History. But I don't think I'll ever make it. Too bad, I'll just have to be philosophical about it. All that by way of saying that after the Black Death, I was in a terrible state. Books were what saved me. I was so ashamed: fancy having been in love with a man who could find a nuclear bureaucrat charming, how uncivilized is that? Since that episode, I've given up for good any thoughts of romance or even fancy. Because if a fancy takes hold of you, it's dangerous, very dangerous. Watch out. I don't know what *you* do to keep going every day, but what I do is recharge my batteries here in my basement. Even though it isn't a very interesting job. If indeed there are any interesting jobs in this profession. Still, some people have better perches than me. Because a library works according to a strict hierarchy. Readers may not realize it, but we're all subject to a pitiless ranking. At the top, in his office, the Head

What could I talk about with women who go to karaoke bars in winter and museums in summer? Not for me. And anyway, to make any impression on this long-standing hierarchy, you'd have to start by making a fuss and there you go, that would stress me. So I stay in my basement, being humiliated. Because it works between sections as well. Not all the classifications are equal. On paper, of course they are, but oh no, not in real life. French Literature and History: they're the blue-blood aristocracy, the nobles at the royal court. And on the same level you have the high society of Philosophy and Religion. Then come the minor gentry in Foreign Languages; with perhaps a bit ahead of them Economics and Social Science: they're the law lords, the legal aristocracy. Just below them, you get the bourgeoisie of periodicals and magazines: all mouth and no action. Alongside that, there's the impregnable citadel of the Children's section – let's call it the lower clergy. Not to mention, because I won't, the open shelves with C.D.s and D.V.D.s, they're the *nouveaux riches*. But *even* lower down, comes the proletariat: Science, Geography, I.T.,

But I know lots of things, I could tell them how to do *their* jobs. One day, for instance, I allowed myself to make a little remark. Since I love Maupassant, I pointed out that the only books of his in the Literature section were his bestsellers: *Boule de Suif, Bel-Ami, Le Horla*. But all his other short stories and books, *Strong as Death, Mont-Oriol*, you can't find them at all, impossible. Same thing for Simone de Beauvoir. Everyone thinks she just wrote *The Second Sex*. Well, she wrote some other great books, excellent novels, but you won't find them up there. So I pointed out to the woman in charge of the ground floor that it was pointless buying bad translations of novels from Uzbekistan that nobody borrows unless you had bought up all the books and novels by Beauvoir and Maupassant, and you know what? She just laughed in my face. Yes, she laughed in my face. A crime against culture, that's what it was. Took me weeks to get over that. Especially since, you may not realize this, it took a really, really big effort to pluck up the courage to go and make that comment. Because I absolutely hate drawing attention to myself, I'm not a natural rebel. But when, for once, I

48

"numbness". Not a word you see often today. But it's a good word to describe the exalted state of the soul, "numbness". This armchair's so comfy, I could almost go to sleep here, this is where you should have slept last night. Personally, I prefer early Maupassant to late Maupassant. Because his later novels are a touch sentimental, I have to say. He'd left the Naval Ministry where he was a civil servant and he'd started to be a successful writer. But going round salons and society hostesses, not all of them very reputable, prancing about, making money, that spoiled him. With his royalties, he bought a sailing boat, a Mediterranean yacht. Big mistake. The beginning of the end. Sailing's no good to anyone, whereas rowing is excellent for keeping fit. He started to fall ill, and he died at forty-three. And here, in this library, we don't even have his complete works. How shaming is that? Whereas Balzac, who was a mass-production writer, someone who pissed out prose, of course they've got the whole lot. *The Human Comedy*, oh, come on, the biggest confidence trick of the century. Balzac wrote to pay off his debts, everyone knows that.

way, I like you, because just now, when you were lying there fast asleep between the bookcases 930 and 940, although it's absolutely against the rules, I didn't have to listen to a lot of apologies from you. On the contrary, you started shouting at me, Very healthy. People apologize too much, everyone's afraid of giving offence and it leads to literature being written for babies. Lowbrow rubbish. That's not the way to become an adult. In September, when the autumn books come out, I see all these stupid titles invading the bookshops, and a few months later they're on the scrap heap. All the hundreds of books pouring off the presses, ninety-nine per cent of them they'd do better to use the paper for wrapping takeaways. And for libraries, it's a disaster. The worst ones are the books on instant history, current affairs: no sooner commissioned than written, printed, televised, bought, remaindered, then taken off the shelves and pulped. The publishers ought to put a sell-by date on them, because they're just consumer goods. No really, the annual crop of autumn books is not my cup of tea. But every September I have to go upstairs to help the be prepared to get rid of the surplus. No more fat. No pity for bad books. When in doubt, chuck it out, that's my motto. But that kind of attitude is finished, over, I'm from the old school now. When you come into this library, what's the first thing you see? Kids wet behind the ears in front of the comic book shelves. And alongside them, Music. Just behind that, D.V.D.s, that's where cultural democracy has got us. It's not a library anymore, with silence reigning over shelves full of intelligence, it's a leisure centre where people come to amuse themselves. At the Ministry of Culture they lap it up, and on high the Head Librarian is perfectly happy. But you know what, Monsieur le Ministre, I've heard all your arguments: make the *médiathèque* a place of pleasure and conviviality in the very heart of the town. Make it less intimidating to go into a library. Blend culture and pleasure so that culture becomes pleasurable – and so on and so on. But it's phoney, all that, it's a lie, it's manipulation. Because culture *isn't* the same thing as pleasure. Culture calls for a permanent effort by the individual to escape the vile condition of an under-civilized primate. Look is deceiving you, you young folk, he knows perfectly well that people don't begin to foster thoughts of revolution when their ears are bombarded by noise, but in the murmuring silence of reading to oneself. But it's too late now. Our shelves are already retreating under their battering rams. Before long they'll create an even deeper level for me, a cellar, and on the ground floor they'll open a café. And on this level, why not a night club while they're at it? That would really bring in the crowds, Monsieur le Ministre. Just one more step to take: develop the hi-tech, expand the *videothèque*, and soon the *médiathèque* will be a *discothèque*, it's bound to happen! Ah, no, what am I saying, it's impossible, I'll never let it come to that. Forgive me if I'm getting worked up, but it's tough being in the minority. I feel like the Maginot Line of public reading. I feel so lonely sometimes, I don't know whether you understand what I'm saying. I doubt it. I'd really like to share all this with Martin. I don't know what his political opinions are. I know so little about him. The only time we had a more personal exchange, what you might call a conversation, was one Tuesday strip lighting on, but it makes a buzz." I threw out this remark to test his taste a bit, to start a conversation – agreed it wasn't very brilliant, but he should have guessed I was flustered. But he just answered: "Oh that doesn't matter, but please, I would prefer more light." And he went back to his seat. I was a bit disappointed. I've often thought about it since. I replay the scene in my head. I ask myself what I should have replied, what he would have said in return, and so on. Don't take this the wrong way, but it's a pity it was you and not Martin that got locked in my basement. If it had been Martin, we could have had highly intellectual conversations, lasting hours and hours, even if it meant ending up exhausted, drained, worn out . . . We would have had a really intelligent exchange. Well, that's not how it worked out. Since that brief conversation, on a December morning, I like winter better. Before, I used to dread it. Winter, you know, is always a bit special. During the really cold months, the library fills up with a lot of desperate people: the homeless, families with young children, dropouts with their plastic bags, it's a real refugee centre. You them and often ask them to be quiet. Not speaking when you're in a group is unnatural, but it's part of learning to be civilized. Except for me. For me, not speaking comes naturally. Well, O.K., today it's different, because you're here, but otherwise, as a rule, I keep my mouth shut. Apart from the students, spring is usually a pretty quiet season. I get bored here with all my shelfmarks in the same place. It gets to me in the end. Sometimes the readers think we're being grumpy towards them. You have to understand us: who'd choose to come and shut themselves up under these neon lights and inside these plasterboard walls when the sun's just starting to send out the first timid rays of warmth and the grass is greening under the wind at lambing time, eh? I ask you. Only damned souls like us, the captives of culture, locked in our silo, who else would let themselves be locked in like this? You can't think how boring it can get. You fill out order slips, the students are revising, I peer up at the blue sky through the windows and think of Martin. In spring, I see much less of him. Not that I'm jealous, that's not the way I am, but something tells me he's in summer. They come here as a sort of exercise, it's kind of like jogging or walking the dog. They need something to do. Some of them ring the changes: they go to the law courts on Tuesdays and Thursdays, when the preliminary hearings are held, and on Wednesdays and Fridays they come to the municipal library. Ah, it's the other way round, is it? If you say so. Well, you get your entertainment where you can. People can be lonely, terribly lonely. Reading's an excuse. A pretext. What they're looking for here is something to hang on to. If you don't believe me, how come you don't even want to go home at night? Who would come and shut themselves up in this basement if they were of sound mind? Yes, go on, admit it, you're a bit borderline yourself. Well, anyway, libraries do attract mad people. Especially in summer. Of course, if you closed the libraries during the summer holidays, you wouldn't see them. No more lunatics, poor people, children on their own, students who've failed their exams, no more little old chaps, no more culture and no more humanity. When I think that some mayors dare to close their libraries in August. Just to cut down on costs. Barbaric. Think of it: when the town's sweltering in the heat, the shops are all shut, the swimming baths are full, people's purses are empty, their pay's too low, and they're brooding over their problems in the shade, with the tar melting on the road, the house of culture could be opening its arms to all those children lost in an ocean of urban idiocy, but no, his nibs the Mayor has closed the library. The bastard. What's the little old pensioner going to do in August? I'll tell you: he gets up on Tuesday morning, he takes the only bus of the day, and he toddles along slowly to the entrance of the library, because for twenty-four hours he's been looking forward to a nice long day spent in an air-conditioned reading room, leafing through his favourite newspapers, and then like a stab in the back, or Napoleon's *coup d'etat*, my poor little pensioner sees the criminal notice on the door: *Closed until September*. And then Durkheim is surprised there are more suicides in summer. It's so sad. Nothing is sadder than an empty library. I mean a library that's open, but with no readers. It can happen, though, in any season. And there we sit, like Uncle Scrooge of their total impotence. In my case, the older I get, the more aware I become of my limits. The older I get, the chances of Martin ever looking at me are shrinking all the time. I know it. Every day spent here takes me a step nearer the grave. Soon it will be over. Not very nice for a man, but for a woman it's even worse. That depresses me. The only thing that consoles me is to be surrounded by people as depressed as I am. The readers down here, they're *seriously* depressed and that cheers me up. You yourself for instance, if I can put this politely, you don't exactly look like a bundle of laughs. No, don't pretend, I can see right through you. You're sad, and lonely. But if you didn't come in here, it'd be worse. No, don't argue, you're absolutely right to come here. You should never just sit around moping at home. When your family's abandoned you, you haven't got any friends, you think you're rubbish, worthless, nothing, books are a great help. Just think about it: what can make human beings suffer more than awareness of their limits? I don't mean fear of death, I mean our suffering at realizing our intelligence is limited. But when we go into a library and look at all those bookcases stretching into the distance, what descends on our soul, if not grace? Spiritually, we can at last fill the terrible emptiness that makes us just worms creeping on this earth. Those endless bookshelves reflect back to us an ideal image, the image of the full range of the human mind. Then all the paths are made plain, everything's newly created once more, and we move closer to a mystical vision of Abundance. The inexhaustible milk of human culture, right here, within our reach. Help yourself, it's free. Borrow, because as much as accumulation of material things impoverishes the soul, cultural abundance enriches it. My culture doesn't stop where someone else's begins. In fact, the library is the place where the greatest solidarity between humans takes place. Humanity, in its most depressing and suffering state, the most beautiful humanity there is, actually, the sinners, the unemployed, the cold weather refugees, they're all around me here. Knock and it shall be opened to you, ask and you shall be served . . . What? You're laughing? Oh good grief, for once I was being serious, and I got carried away again. But you're right, let me his legs. Who's sorry now? His telephone's stopped ringing. Suddenly, he has all the time in the world. So he'll come and start flipping through the pages of the newspapers and realize he doesn't know anything about public affairs – he'll be amazed at our new system that lets you borrow books for six weeks at a time, renewable once. His wife will leave him, he'll become obsessive or depressed, he'll start playing boules, and even become a pedestrian. He'll be one of us. But it will have taken all those body-blows from life for him to understand that the library, that building he used to go past with utter indifference, doesn't hold a lot of dead books, no, it's the beating heart of the Great Consolation. I'd go further. What do you think all this represents, the welcoming arms of the bookshelves, the soft carpets underfoot, the restful semi-silence, the warm temperature, the discreet and benevolent supervision? You can't guess? Don't be afraid to say what you think. Let me remind you, I'm completely neutral towards you, and anything we say in this room won't go beyond these four walls. You still don't get it? But it's obvious. Going into the library my watch gone? Here's something else. My jewellery. Some earrings. I hide them in a drawer and I put them on discreetly when I see Martin arrive. You don't catch flies with vinegar, as my mother would say. Poor woman: she's never read a book in her life, but on that subject she's a walking encyclopedia. And if I'd listened to her, I would have kept a closer eye on the Black Death and the radioactive fallout from the nuclear power station. She did warn me, my mother. Watch out, she said. One never does watch out enough. You trust people, you go with the flow, you drop off to sleep, and oops, there you are in a basement all night. I'm teasing you. You're lucky it was a week night, or you might have spent the whole weekend in here, starving to death. Oh, here's my watch. Excuse me, I have to do a few things, we'll be opening soon. It's not all set up yet. The trolleys have to be emptied, it all has to look neat and tidy. Even if, between ourselves, most people have no idea of all I've been telling you, what goes on here. Most readers don't come for the good of their soul. Some of them don't come to borrow books, or to work, not even to read . . .

phone number. Now don't tell the Librarian, but I wrote underneath, *Mature woman would like to meet young man who admires Critique of Dialectical Reason for Sartrean adventure.* Obviously, not everyone would get it. And nobody ever replied. Admittedly, I didn't dare put my phone number. But I don't see why I shouldn't have a bit of fun too, instead of watching the readers getting off with each other and the books stacking up. I've got a right to something, haven't I? I don't see why, since I'm neither more nor less depressed than anyone else, I should have to spend my whole life not being noticed. My whole life, down in this basement. Martin, I know perfectly well, never looks at me. He's totally indifferent to me. And yet I do everything I can to make it nice here. I've had armchairs brought in, I got hold of a pot plant. You don't see many of those in libraries. Perhaps Martin doesn't like rubber plants. I don't know what I have to do to get his attention. Put a note in with his borrower's slip? I can't offer him a bunch of flowers! Such a lovely neck . . . No, never, he never so much as looks at me. He just sits there reading his old history books, that really gets the chance to come and swell our groaning bookshelves, and every year they make me more aware of my limited span, my old age and my insignificance. Yes. It's all an illusion, a massive illusion. You never feel so miserable as in a library. You can bow down in front of books all you like, try to understand, read and re-read them, but there's no hope. You know this perfectly well. Books can't do anything for us. They will always win out. In fact, if you don't keep trying to hold the lid down on them, they'll kill us all, the damn things. They have their own logic. Remember, last month? There was an armchair here and four reader's seats. All gone. Replaced by two bookcases made of chipboard, for shelfmark 960. The counter-revolution is under way. We have to do something. Their aim is the elimination of all readers from the library. I can see the books planning it. They hold meetings, they pile up in towers, they barricade themselves in the stores, and once they've gathered enough strength, they charge. With the help of some of the librarians, the aristos on the staff, they're getting the best places, bit by bit. The readers step back, stumble, resist a little, but gradually get pushed out, they're in the way, human beings are in the way, and they know it. So, in the end, they throw up their hands and leave. That's it. *Finito*, "The dead eat up the living" as the old saying goes. I'll tell you how it works. The library is the arena where every day the Homeric battle between books and readers begins. In this struggle, the librarians are the referees. In this arena, they have a part to play. Either they're cowards and take the side of the mountain of books, or they bravely help the worried reader. And in this fight, you have to let your conscience be your guide. But librarians aren't automatically on the side of the humans, don't be fooled. You don't realize, but you're a flock of sheep in our hands, you think you're gambolling about free as air, but there are wolves everywhere lying in wait for you, cyclops, sirens, naked nymphs, oh, the pity of it . . . A barricade only has two sides and I know which side I'm on, comrade. I'm here to help the poor, depressed, thirsty reader faced with the crushing prestige of the Army of Books. You haven't noticed, because I keep myself to myself, but I'm on your side and always aren't on their side. When you've always been useless at school, thousands of books all gathered together in one place are scary, humiliating, for a man they're castrating – well, that's by the by. So, now my little flock settles down. That's when you have to go over to them with a big smile and welcome them. They've got a project to do for school. I bring them some books. They whisper to each other, they don't sit still. The regulars give them dirty looks, but it's not too bad. Then some of them come back. They start to know their way around. They read pretty useless books, but at least they're reading. It can take months, this kindness offensive. We know we've won when they come back all on their own. That's when they feel at home, they're accepted, they're reassured. They have a right to be here. "School sometimes makes mistakes, and the library can put them right," that's what Eugène Morel said. Ah . . . Eugène. Ah . . . Martin. Yes, indeed, you can accomplish great things if you're a librarian. That's why I really can't understand why Martin is so indifferent towards me. O.K., I didn't get the right grades for the teaching certificate, but still, I'm not so bad, am I? Answer, please. What does this kid want? To meet an I.T. manageress? A woman who puts the banknotes in A.T.M.s? A woman who sells private swimming pools? A nuclear power station engineer? No, I really don't get it. Here I am doing a useful, interesting and brave job, one that calls for a whole lot of qualities. When they bring a book back: "Yes, I liked that one too, did you?" Point out another they might like. Gently ease them away from the bestseller shelves. Apply emotional tactics. Agreed, they don't always work. I may not be that good at it. But I could say in my defence that it all depends on what's gone before. At the very beginning. Everything depends on the very first days, the first time someone walks over the threshold. That's when it starts. The beginnings of civilization. Birth. The primal scene. Before that, frankly, the reader is a virgin. Yes, a virgin. And I like to see people losing their library cherry. Oh well, of course, if the first time is a fiasco, it'll be hard to carry on. Very hard. If the librarian comes charging at you like a bull, no kindness, no foreplay, that's it. You'll never come back. Divorced from culture. Lifelong

Then you have to wait. And waiting already sets you up for humiliation. Your desire for the book gets blunted, and by the time the book arrives the reader has gathered that nobody cares about his enthusiasm. They've arranged everything it takes to put people off for life, to cause immense frustration. Of course, after that, I can't pick up the pieces, the damage has been done. Not to mention that a traumatic system like this leads to the development of library neurosis, repression on a grand scale, and before you know it, outbreaks of sex attacks and cultural violence, I don't have to draw a diagram, do I? Oh, hear that noise? They're winding the blinds up. The doors will be open soon. I'd better put my earrings on, you never know. I'm going to confess something to you. About the back of his neck. No, I've had plenty of time to think about it, haven't I, so I've thought about it a lot. This other evening, I was at my desk. I had this book in my hands and I was just going to re-shelve it. A solid sort of book, a hardback with a nice squared spine. And as I was putting it into place, I looked at it again, among the others. And seen from the back, this book reminded me of something, but what? And then, I kid you not, I had this revelation. It was the back of Martin's neck. Yes. Then I understood. What's the spine of a book, if not its nape? No need to look at me like that, anyone can see you don't spend your life among people and books with their backs turned on you. Well, this flash of insight just blew my mind. Now, even looking at that bookcase, I sometimes get a funny feeling . . . The worst thing is when Martin is wandering around among the books. All I have to do is get up, and pretend I've got something to sort out. I can follow him quite closely. I try to sneak along a few steps behind him. And that's when I get the most beautiful sight of all: the back of Martin's neck, a kind of synthesis, a universal résumé of Man's inviolate buttocks, wandering through hundreds of books all with *their* backsides turned towards you, and the two buttocks multiplied infinitely and magnified by the nape of Martin's neck, it makes me want to, well, I don't know what I might be capable of. But not in the Town Planning and Geography section, no, it's completely impossible. Now don't you go telling the Head Librarian that, eh? I don't finally dealt with all its traumas and sexual hang-ups. Because in the end that's all writers ever think about. Take Maupassant, for instance: he went mad before he died. After *Le Horla*, the critics churned out pages of stuff about how it displayed existential angst which had been there since his childhood, and a repressed dual personality, and so on and so on. Oh, give me a break! The truth is that Maupassant died from the final brain lesions resulting from a case of syphilis that wasn't properly treated. Maupassant was sexually obsessed. Remember the night he got Flaubert, plus some official, to stand witness that he could have sex with six women of the night in one hour? Away to the whorehouse, under starter's orders, and they're off! Great role model, wouldn't you say? Anyway, Maupassant said, "Bel-Ami, that's me." And *Bel-Ami* isn't a satire on the world of journalism, as they say in those textbooks for provincial schoolchildren. *Bel-Ami* isn't even a novel, it's an ode to male potency as a weapon of domination, allied to money. How exemplary is that? And what about Balzac, eh? A man who spends his time in his dressing-gown, drinking

loves, all that blarney, oh, she suffered, poor Simone . . .
No, Martin prefers to flirt with his blonde. Yes, there's a
blonde in the frame – the other day she even dared ask
me a question, oh I wasn't going to help *her*, worse than
an architect . . . Nobody will say this, but take it from me
– Beauvoir used to throw these jealous tantrums with
Sartre, but he wouldn't budge an inch. Like Martin.
Whatever I try, he never so much as looks at me . . . So
when he went chasing after some other woman, Simone
had to copy him. But it was because she was miffed. And
I understand . . . So what am *I* supposed to do? Try and
get off with one of the warehousemen? Bring in another
rubber plant? Borrow some D.V.D.s? . . . It's pitiful. There
was a lot of talk about the American, Nelson Algren,
Simone had an affair with. But it was Sartre who started
it. When he was in the States, the great philosopher fell
for some little American tootsie. So what do you expect,
poor Simone was bound to feel abandoned . . . I can see
him now, Martin, chatting about Madame de Pompadour
with his blonde hussy . . . So of course, being miffed,
Beauvoir found herself a transatlantic oddball, look at

hear something now . . . Yes, they're opening up. You can go upstairs now and get out. I'm truly sorry for what happened. But please, don't go repeating anything I said. I feel a bit ashamed now. You mustn't take it literally. It was just, you know, a flight of fancy. It isn't always easy to stay put, you have to do what you can. You caught me unawares and sometimes in this prison, with all the books, something's got to give. Yes, some days it feels like I could die down here and nobody would notice. People don't know where the library is. They walk by without seeing me. Ungrateful lot. I've never got a word of thanks from Martin, my refugees, my little old men, my school dunces. Once they leave here, they forget about me. I'm stuck in my basement, while the duchesses upstairs are giggling. When I get home at night, I can't even bring myself to read. And yet it all starts up again every day. I fall for it. The Homeric struggle. Every day, I go back into the arena. Every dayI say to myself: What if he doesn't come? What if all is lost? What good will it have been to put shelf-marks on all these books? What good will it have been